The J Girls

BLUE LIGHT BOOKS

The J Girls

A Reality Show

INDIANA UNIVERSITY PRESS

Indiana Review

BLUE LIGHT BOOKS

This book is a publication of

Indiana University Press
Office of Scholarly Publishing
Herman B Wells Library 350
1320 East 10th Street
Bloomington, Indiana 47405 USA
iupress.org

Indiana Review
Bloomington, Indiana

Cover art by Anni Jyn

Manufactured in the United States of America

First Printing 2022

Cataloging information is available from the Library of Congress.

ISBN 978-0-253-06060-0 (paperback)
ISBN 978-0-253-06061-7 (ebook)

For all the girls I've been & known

One finds or invents an identity only by staging it, making fun of it, entertaining it, throwing it—as the ventriloquist throws the voice, wisecracks projected into a mannequin's mouth.

WAYNE KOESTENBAUM

Contents

The J Girls

Preface

The following footage was recovered from a set of three VHS tapes found at a community rummage sale in the basement of St. Agnes Catholic Church in Gaudeville, Ohio. Organized by the City of Gaudeville as part of its 2020 Revitalization Plan, the sale consisted largely of items cleared from nearby abandoned homes that were slated for demolition. These tapes were labeled *The J Girls: A Reality Show* and marked with the years 1997, 1998, and 2000. They were accompanied by a small collection of notebooks and folders containing incomplete notes on *The J Girls*, including a handwritten cast list. The tapes and notes were purchased for one dollar by a local resident and subsequently transcribed for the county library archives.

Abbreviations Used

INT   Interior
EXT   Exterior
VO   Voice-over
OC   Off camera

Cast List

SETTING: Gaudeville, Ohio 1997–2000

JOCELYN as HERSELF (Age 14–17)
Bootlegs cosmetics to pay for tattoos from her dream-sleeve list;
Spawn of a Maui Lounge mermaid and an MIA boozehound—not missed.

JODIE as HERSELF (Age 16–19)
Drives a sweet-ass Chevy she bought with Taco Bell paychecks;
Takes the long way home to avoid Mom's men and wrecks.

JENNIFER as HERSELF (Age 16–19)
Addicted to soap operas and Nair;
Speaks mostly in pulp and prayer.

JACQUI as HERSELF (Age 15–18)
College hungry, read half of *The Feminine Mystique*;
Her goddess tarot deck says she's about to peak.

JOELLE as HERSELF (Age 13–16)
Jodie's sister—stoner rink rat with a deadbeat dad;
Wears flame tights and Doc Martens under Catholic plaid.

JACQUI'S MOM as HERSELF (Age 36–39)
Night nurse who needs a beer;
Doesn't want to be here.
                    Single! *(written in the margin)*

ANONYMOUS WOMAN in VARIOUS ROLES
Nobody you can see;
A safer name than *me*.

Opening Credits

*MONTAGE. Close shots of the items described with alternating VO from all five
J GIRLS.*

Adoration of the J Girls

Jocelyn, Jodie, Jennifer, Jacqui, Joelle: Gaudeville girl-gods of quick
fingers and full pockets. The J Girls, who lap the block garbed in
exaltation:
Jocelyn of black thongs and push-ups swapped out in dressing
rooms. Jodie of Oxy-filled purses and money to hide. Jennifer of sweater-
swaddled kittens from behind garage doors. Jacqui of sleeved Slim Jims
and pregnancy tests. Joelle of white cutoffs and lilac-bruised thighs.

The J Girls who pool-hop apartments to christen each other bikini-
clad diehards. The J Girls who laugh in spirals and slather themselves
with joy:
Jocelyn of blue eyeliner and numbers scrawled on her palm. Jodie
of chlorine-green hair and lipstick swiped from the drugstore. Jennifer of
translucent eyelids and cheeks stained self-tanner orange. Jacqui of Kool-
Aid-dyed bangs and henna-etched arms. Joelle of mascara freckles and a
double dimple on one side.

The J Girls who breathe chains of smoke Os from the blessed flames of
their mouths and cough together in rounds:
Jocelyn of gold-ringed thumbs
and Newport 100s. Jodie of hemp bracelets and spliffed Camel Wides.
Jennifer of turquoise nails and Virginia Slims. Jacqui of silver star anklets
and Salem Full Flavor 85s. Joelle of the filched Zippo and trembling
Marlboro Ultra Lights.

The J Girls who gospel in gossip of plush tongues and soft-slurred
consonants and bent-backed vowels. The J Girls who know more than
they spill:
Jocelyn of pink pig-latin love notes to girls. Jodie of the hot dad
who got caught jacking cars. Jennifer of married cousins in Springfield.

Jacqui of the Ms. mom who smokes pot on her porch. Joelle of the recurring stepfather curse.

The J Girls who reign extreme in the kingdom of making do:

Jocelyn, queen of hearts in juvie. Jodie, queen of flea-bombed carpets and snarling yard mutts. Jennifer, queen of the west-side babysitting ring. Jacqui, queen of beaded doorways and leaky waterbeds and torn Naugahyde. Joelle, queen of lonesome skinny-dipped midnights.

The omnipotent J Girls, who swim circles through shame. The J Girls who say *no duh, no really, no jinx, no takebacks, no fair, no shit, not sorry, not dead, not hardly, not long but not never, whatever, not finished, not enough, not yet.*

EPISODE 1

The J Girls Get High

(1997)

Monologue: Jocelyn

INT. SCHOOL CAFETERIA – DAY. JOCELYN stands in an empty cafeteria wearing a red tube top and a silver miniskirt. Posters hang on the wall behind her: "Reduce, Reuse, Recycle"; the "Hang in There" kitten; a diagram of a cartoon girl that illustrates proper skirt length and notes, "All hair colors must come directly from God"; a flyer for Modesty Club, on which someone has drawn a vulva.

Less Is More

We fast through lunch & pocket pills at recess.
Gold letters on our gym-class asses crown us
each a *Princess*.
    School nuns scold, so we dig
little graves in our minds & they fill them
with etiquette. Bet they'll better us yet.
        In church,
our voices rise, a sour choir of spit & pride. We stir
the nuns' words in our mouths till they curdle:
less is more.
    At home, our mean mothers pour
Suave into Avon bottles, stacking dimes as we lie
like strips of jerky on our roofs.
        We tan. We turn.
We cure ourselves & wonder: How far down
our throats can these new woman hands go?

Together we trace rows of looping red Xs & Os
into our arms with paring knives. We carve our skin
to the bone,
    becoming instruments of less—
but we make it up in excess: rhinestone eyelids,
two-inch acrylics, hair frosted in three tones.

Each hotbox ride with garage boys is a fantasy
of proving the nuns right:
                         we see the road stop
like a cartoon cliff & we're driving on air till
someone looks down & we drop & that's all
we've wanted.
               To hell with other kids' futures,
our parents' tired *rising above*.
                      A new high:
the long whistle of wind like a lullaby
against the slicked reeds of these whittled bodies
as we fall glittering to the bottom.

Monologue: Jodie

EXT. CHURCH FESTIVAL – DAY. JODIE sits at a picnic table. JENNIFER sits next to her, eating cotton candy and nodding. Beside the table is a garbage can overflowing with paper plates, soda cans, cigarette packs, and half-eaten funnel cakes. Dried nacho cheese trails down the side of the can, and a few yellow jackets hover.

Wifebeaters

A shirtless rack makes a cozy hang for beatings
if a girl's hard-pressed or steamed. Words get worn
this way: at festivals, we tuck our violence in
our bras with cash for cigarettes and pretzels.
Neon sparks in spacious skulls—girlness is a gas
to tap, so we trap its heat against our breasts

and vent little whines when the Zipper cage flips us.
Whipped fright froths our kid lips, and we run
our mouths at the carnie hand-humping his lever
below. He holds us catawampus to better glimpse
our tits while shouts burst bright on blacktop sky.
For future wives, there is only coming down

from here, so we best burn serotonin slow
and tamp fissures with new clothes. Fashion
schools us: a slut can wear her insides out,
but sleevelessness is also cloak. Walmart magic:
black straps like tongues ventriloquize sex
into cotton undershirts—but if a boy sees

his own skivvies, it may be triggered fists. Still,
we tempt a hit, prepared to temper it with sheer force
of this half-flash. Soap won't wash the bull's-eyes off
our backsides, so why not don the darts ourselves?
Mimicry's a prizeless game, but anyway,
the board is always rigged—even girls know that.

Monologue: Jennifer

INT. CHURCH – DAY. JENNIFER stands in front of a marble altar and large wooden crucifix, holding a bag of communion hosts and drinking from a silver wine goblet.

Prayer for Effacement

O my fear-snuffer, my sensitive sigh-huffer,
my infernal grace-breather, my sin-sucker,
my most holy vampire, my tawdry tear-drinker,
my gory grief-strainer, my pulpy vice-eater,
my dull mind-cleaver, my gentle heart surgeon,
my acid bath, my quick-drying limewash,
my most patient primer, my tongue-scrape,
my meticulous airbrush, my aerial light box,
my traveling sunspot, my beautiful cataract,
my personal snow machine, my salt-n-plow,
my spongy ink-blotter, my stack of *sorry*s,
my emergency stain stick, my cup of bleach,
my benevolent eraser—make me an eternal
thumbprint, your most stubborn spot of grease.

Monologue: Jacqui

*EXT. PLAYGROUND – DUSK. JACQUI sits on a lawn chair in the grass and holds a
can of Natural Light, from which she never drinks, instead waving it around for emphasis.*

Middling

At half past nine, this park is a palace
of teenage bombast & angst-gilded crime.
  Too proud to be vandals, we hike & heel
half miles at a time. Into the woods we go,
  packing spliffs & a beer & half a line
of this boy's blow. He splits it all with me
  because I'm *chill*, though I know it's because
I live uptown, straddling the tracks. His hands
  flit & shimmer like ghosts around his face
as he rants about dads & cops & class.
  His lips are aneurysms in my eye,
so when he says my name, I go half-blind
  & he half-jokes that our joint is laced
with angel dust. *Lovely name*, I say & unswallow
  all the air I'll need for a lifetime. We weep
laughter on our backs. Our throats are flutes
  for calling half thoughts back to our bodies.
Gold lid-lacquer seeps into my pupils & the clouds
  pulse with my blood's half beats. I slip
from my sleeves, pull my jeans to my knees.
  In this dead time, I make my own sublime.
I'm halfway toward happy, finally, so I sing
  to my meddling mom: Come to me with college
dreams. Come to me with scholarships & church
  & two-car garages housing shiny husbands.
Come to me with every half-uttered *almost*
  clogging your mouth like a mulch of dead leaves.
Come scatter them now at my muddy bare feet.

Monologue: Joelle

EXT. BACKYARD – SUNSET. JOELLE and JOCELYN sit cross-legged on the grass.

Thigh High

A contact buzz—muscular twitch
beyond the suede itch of looking

at a constellation of blue veins
under ice. Sometimes desire

says *break it,* so I lay a hand on you
with a laugh, with a *girl, I know.*

Your tiny hairs catch like breaths
on my finger grooves. Razor burn

blooms like specks of fire and spreads
through goose bumps, little triggers.

I want to test you. You let me
press your ink and citrus bruises,

and it's nearly enough. I phantom grip
your stretch marks like electric currents

between my teeth at night. Desire
is a far cry from the men's palms

that cup our thighs without asking:
touch as a collar to say *mine.*

Once, two boys flanked us walking,
asking each other whether

they liked our legs better jiggling
or still. We both giggled, but

I thought: What do they know
about gravity. The sky bowed

behind you all afternoon, waiting
for permission. Girl, you

are a hall of mirrors falling on me—
you are the end of looking. I crush

my eyes to crumbs, and you dizzy them
to the ground, the softest shattering.

Monologue: Jacqui

INT. BEDROOM – NIGHT. JACQUI stands at a microphone in front of a closet door. She is wearing a hot-pink wig and matching pink sneakers.

Ode on My Upspeak

I admire its belligerent uncertainty—
I'll know if I know when I please. Pointed
indecision as autoprick that sticks my sentence-tip.
When my tongue spring-toes into a run, I vault
across silences, sucking this tick like perpetual mint—
surprised but satisfied. I want all my action
rising, okay? While we're at it, I dig my *umm*s,
impervious little monks who squat
in well-spaced rows, their insistent vibrato
a hypnochant that spins my speech to incantation.
I love how they punctuate, bead-like,
my vocal fry, that holey string to which I cling.
Its creak makes me speak like a crumb scraper
savoring the linen tablecloth. I lick
the conversation down and shake
each glottal rattle at the sky, my diphthong
kernels popping in a thrum that sets me singing
like an optimist—I've got nowhere to go but up.

Commercial Break: Jocelyn

INT. BEDROOM – NIGHT. JOCELYN sits on a made bed with a zebra bedspread, five spray bottles lying next to her. As she says the name of each fragrance, she holds up the corresponding bottle, tilts her head to one side, and sprays the body mist on her neck, never breaking eye contact with the camera.

Bath & Body Works Pastoral

I. Cucumber Melon

Reluctant virgins, we'd kill for a clue. We're foul with ambition and clunky in pumps. Joelle fronts cool, but we cook up hot with no warning, man crazy, so we douse fire with sugared perfume. Voilà:

near-men—or near-misses— drop with sudden nakedness like nukes. Fueled, their sex mushrooms. When we talk condoms and birth control, our words melt in utero. Already we're embers. We burn red and low. At fourteen,

we're numbered honeys to them, though they call us cute because we're limber and new. We are girls in lieu—of women, of cash, of real plunder. Love-encumbered, we let them do. They sell us on petty bets for dry petting, but our want is whet for felons. We need

a grand thieving. All year, we plan and smolder under the lid of dumb youth. We feed flares with bottled guile. We curse our unquiet brains, our not-quite heft, our cumbersome ruin coming.

II. Juniper Breeze

A Johnny arrives like the greenest June, a noontide of heat inside. His breath is a sun brine that soaks me till I'm speckled weak. I grate his gaze against my skin and wait for it to pare me. Teeth stir my zeal for fantasy:

a tipped-back head is a bite is a rip in my throat is a ripened sigh is a night that breathes soft bees right through me. You know—pins and feeble knees.

His twin bed

proves me at first a zipper tease, but his urgency cinches my lips and fissures *no* into *yes*, consent sinking in as I carry home a seething seed of *no* in my jeans. But I fix my story up quick for friends,

selling them on my own appetite: I wanted it, I wanted it. I flavor myself with want, little dabs at the elbows and neck. Joelle's intoxicated by it, so I wrap myself in her jealousy and smother my truth in something sweet.

III. Country Apple

For weeks, I kept it up. Johnny said I was a nonesuch, a country pleasure, an uncounted bounty in the bedroom—but fickle lips sucked me dry. Done now,

he makes the rounds, calling me a cored whore. In my head, a mowed clearing two counties wide. My body pastoral. My body past prime. Word in the air is

I'm overripe. Even Joelle collects herself from my side. Wanton is a rotten role. I ferment in time: spite as moonshine. Meanwhile, quaint gossip germinates, and the whole town comes

for a slice. Swallowed pride as turned tide: they eat me up and I'm savored as ever, a favorite *Oh my,* sour speck in their collective eye.

IV. Pearberry

A bed of sheared familiars makes a comfy place to wild. I'm her: the daredevil, the polecat, the workhorse. And I'm here: the beehive, the woodshed, the doghouse. Every name adheres. I'm an alchemical compound made of favorite fucknouns. What's best

is a pit bull with a mouse mouth, so I play the nice hybrid and nibble my slobber gums when their girlfriends come. I can't bite the shorthand that feeds me, but I can roughhouse on command— faulty loyalty of mutts. What I need

is my own devotee, a whistle-come. I train Joelle in puppy love. Boys are the leash that ties her to me, a proxy cock I swing because a tongue is a tongue and she laps me up. We play soft at catcalls and backbites. Soon we're a duo:

two on one, we chicken with two-timing boys. We sniff them in and work them over, gut for goodies, then pull the wishbones out—souvenirs we can both hold at one time.

V. Plumeria

Joelle and I are a pair of lures now—two lips on the silent slit of night. We open, we close, we purse against each other. Desire licks and we pluralize. We off with our girlskins and cloak our heads in dares, in plumage of dip-dyed hair. When the foxes sleep,

we find them. We pry open the fevered dark, finding boys in every corner, their bellies empty, their tongues red-rare. Nothing but kits, they mewl and empty themselves as we drink up their stage fright. Nullified delight. Then a leakage, outsized:

hysteria on the block—a wary eye blinks into two and two and two more. Parents grow weary of our gilded wrists and ears, our aesthetic of plenty. They think rumors will pâté us thin, but we aim to get stuffed first. We aim to marry up first. We aim to get ours and theirs.

EPISODE 2

The J Girls Chase Tail
(1997)

Monologue: Jodie

INT/EXT. CAR – DAWN. JODIE sits in the driver's seat facing a camera positioned in the passenger seat. Two pink fuzzy dice hang from the rearview mirror, along with Mardi Gras beads and a Powerpuff Girls air freshener.

Ode to My '81 Chevy Celebrity

You're the sapphire runt in our junker rotation, a family
gaudy and fleeting as carnival fish, doomed
as each gem-body lapping toward toilet-bowl death.

Oversized nonetheless, you room out inside
and expose a gut glutted on sticky dimes and Newport butts.
You teach *swallow* in lieu of *clean,* since nobody gripes a free ride

or dares groom a steel trap lined in velveteen.
You droop roof and strut rude sputter in your need,
though we're only poor when we say so. A car to name

is enough for some, but I borrow my deadbeat's in-this-boat trope
and crown myself unlucky—not unto leaving, but unto
griefspoons beneath seats and bitter froth in parking lots.

Unto unzipped jeans. Reach-me-down hoopty, we break easy
in changing hands. Night-stranded, we're silent under hood
but cough cordial amends when dressed in fresh dawn.

Both sixteen, we twin dim heads and cloudy rear-views,
collect red wounds on our underbellies where the world eats through.
Why should a body be this badly made for carrying?

Engine through floor might make for relief.
But death drive's too obvious, so I opt for auto-harm:
gashes tease jilted keys and flaunt a mantle of damage
almost untouchable in its self-loathing.

(Camera is set at ground level, facing empty street.)

JOELLE *(OC): Did you see Dad's letter?*
JODIE *(OC): Yeah, what the fuck was that about?*
JOELLE *(OC): Can you even get married in prison?*
JODIE *(OC): I am not going.*
JOELLE *(OC): Hell no.*
JODIE *(OC): Are those my jeans?*

Monologue: Jacqui's Mom

INT. LIVING ROOM – DAY. JACQUI'S MOM sits cross-legged on a taupe vinyl couch holding a magazine in her lap. She seems to be reading cue cards behind the camera. JACQUI'S school photo in a silver frame is propped on the end table next to her, along with an ashtray shaped like Florida.

Weeknight

Homebound at dawn or dusk, we grip our keys
like ladies: tips out between knuckles
so our fists sprout spikes. Finger of night,
we ask, come stroke something feral inside:
sand-tooth, lemon-tongue, gravel-gut, cayenne-eye.

We clutch desire in our lips and crumple it,
jerking our necks at every cough or scuffle.
See how we shut ourselves up like a dare
to prove we never wanted it—never licked
a dribble of want, never let our tongues roll out.

Watch how we push the honey from our mouths.
How we forget longing and the blooming hands
that feed it to us at home. Look how stiff we are,
our men remark, when we finally arrive.

> JACQUI's MOM *(pulls a purple leather cigarette purse from between two couch cushions, takes out an extralong cigarette, lights it, then slowly exhales smoke through her nostrils):* Okay?
> JAQUI *(OC):* Okay, we might do one more take.
> JACQUI'S MOM: Jesus fucking—

Monologue: Jennifer

INT. CHURCH – DAY. JENNIFER sits in an empty church pew with a stained-glass window depicting the Annunciation behind her.

Prayer for Containment

O my luscious muzzle, my savory switch,
my lamentful lasso, my steadfast fist-clench,
my deepest saddle, my most radial embrace,
my omnipresent invisible electric fence,
my sacred seat belt, my staid straitjacket,
my salvation shackle, my steely soul brace,
my plaster body cast, my stiff tongue girdle,
my moral corset, my reinforced bootstrap,
my airtight Tupperware, my vacuum seal,
my sinproof sippy cup, my locked joybox,
my padded prayer cell, my permanent womb,
my bolted confessional booth—your grace
is my dank crawl space, a tender lion's jaw
where I startle and quiver, your eternal hiccup.

Monologue: Jacqui

INT. KITCHEN – DAY. JACQUI sits cross-legged in a chair with an open dictionary on her lap. She holds her index finger over her lips and slowly runs it down her chest and onto the page as she speaks.

Ode to the C Word

Crude synecdoche, it's a mouthful
of curse that quickens blood
but tickles me. I lick its consonants
like candy. It's fun to bite into
the crisp *ck* and trigger the gust
of *uh* on my tongue, then savor
the slow warmth of *nnn*
against my front teeth, all
for the electric spark of the *t*—
not closure so much as catalyst
for a round of gasps—good
as lifting my skirt. It's intimate:
Listener, let me lay your ear
where I sit. Quaint quagmire,
saucy autotune, cute magic spell—
if I name it, I name myself and come
alive with dirty chatter. Self-satisfied,
my glossy lips won't quiet now.
I could chew this cuss all night.

Monologue: Joelle

INT. SKATING RINK – NIGHT. JOELLE stands in the center of the roller-skating rink in her socks. Above her, a disco ball spins slowly—to little effect, since the overhead lights are on.

The Birth of Anger at the Roller-Skating Rink

This waxed rink is a galaxy of spit-shined teeth
    and sweat-sheened half-globes of padded breasts.
We glide on wheels toward nothing in particular,
    our pinkies vibrating as we pass one another.
Boys with the heavy hands of men line the outer edge,
    so still and preened in flashy caps and jackets
they blend into the neon carpeting. My man is a moon
    brooding in the corner. I let him inside me last night
and then said *stop*, my mind scratching like a record
    as I lay in his bed and watched him finish in me
from some far horizon in my head, so he told his friends:
    too big anyway, too loose—a whisper that echoes
girl to girl in this rink where I am, most nights,
    too small to be seen. Even my first kiss came
like an accidental slap from a strange man, who,
    on his way across this very room to the arcade
or concession stand, tripped over me like a dropped
    candy box and decided he wanted a piece, so took it.
The rumor of my size now bounces around the rink,
    veering fiery toward me, and when it finally hits,
I am ready to shatter into a pile of shimmering dust
    like the kind I find at the bottom of my makeup bag.
If anything happens after death, I pray, let my body
    turn to that. But a bang can birth a great beginning:
I break from our phalanx of denim legs and pivot inward.
    Reeling, I gather speed as gravity follows me.
Girls attach like distant planets, their open mouths strobing
    with laughter. They can't look away from me,

now in the innermost ring. Magnetic, I absorb their luminous
    attention, becoming my own solar system
of gold plating: two hoops, choker chain, four rings orbiting
    my face in perfect time with the wane and gape
of my red aperture as it births a light that obscures all but its own
    glowering. I burn a girl-sized hole in the hissing air
and rise, a mascaraed god-eye, taking in pain unflinching.
    Huge, I spin imperceptibly, turning little by little
toward an orange rage that will, I can see, eclipse everything.

Interview: Anonymous Woman

INT. BASEMENT – NIGHT. ANONYMOUS WOMAN sits on the edge of a waterbed.

VO: *Lorena Bobbitt's defense attorney, Lisa Kemler, has said, "This case was not about a penis."*

The Cut

The fantasy was a blot
on my cornea, indelible red
in the morning mush bowl.
Where did it come from? Surely not
my own impossible head,
always burning & yet whole.

Visualize it—not the act
(blood is old hat for women) but his
orphaned scrap—soft folds silver
with moon & waiting in a field
purpled with night, the itch & prick
of grass conjuring a ghost of heat as nerves
try to stir beneath a canopy of ravenous gnats.

The next day, simple gore of another dawn—
the sun's cruel hush of white like a blanket
on the smoldering pink. What did they want me to say?
The too-human slump of the oblivious
clouds cast a reminder: god is already stuffed
with regrets. With the little morsel
in my hand, I still felt him on top of me.

After an ordeal, panic congeals
at the back of the tongue. Almost sweet
in the morning—you can spread it
like jam across your toast. This I know.

I used to fall asleep sucking on prayer
like a kerosene lozenge each night.
But in bed I didn't dare
unhinge my flaming jaw before God,
who finally said to me:
metaphor will not do.

Shame Soap: Jennifer

MONTAGE. Shots of party scene and items described with VO from JENNIFER.

Origins & Outcomes

a tendency toward men: a tenuous inborn thread: a tangled-up head: a cute little clot: a bad cell caught: the best-laid bloodlines: a gold mine: a land mine: stepped over a thousand times: love like a waltz above it: a tango: a two-step: a soft pet: a petty crime: a crimson drop: a polka-dot skirt: a murder flirt: a flippant hurt: a hint: a sullen shiv: a stitch sewn inside: a new place to hide: a fleshy flowering of red: a chiffon dread: hot little dress: ripped from a party: fabric fit for a hit: an execution: a staged constellation of one: a sorry star: sold to the crowd: thesaurus of sighs: dead weight in the mouth: tiny canker of guilt: burnt tongue of time: a terse little prayer: a chewed-up pit: self-pitying cry: a cut-up curse: a canopy bed: an unborn thread: a homemade hearse: a tendency shed

Commercial Break: Jocelyn

INT. LIVING ROOM – NIGHT. JOCELYN sits on a floral couch holding a red pleather purse. As she says the name of each lip balm flavor, she pulls a new stick out of her purse, and then she applies the balm and licks her lips in an exaggerated circle.

Lip Smacker Fantasia

I. Bubblegum

Glum nuns class our sex with a lesson on mastication risks. Once chomped, they warn, Chiclets lose form—and every desk I jam my pink wad under is another hole in my belt. Does my gummy blob look fat stretched out? And does blowing count? All the girls wonder. My own sour reverie makes for sticky chewing: What if I wasn't quite awake? What if no one believed me anyway? Maybe not so tricky: no takebacks, they say. So I just swallow the past intact. Did you know, the girls ask, that it takes your body seven years to dissolve a gut-lump like that?

II. Dr. Pepper

Desolate means of measure call for desperate medicine dressed as pleasure. Determined to secure a proper popping this time, I shave off my shy parts and rub a burn into my skinny lips—nicks to plump me. Which way for a bitter taste to best sink in—long-savored or quick-changed? Either way, a spoonful of pain is remedy if I can feed it back to them. The ailment is congenital, but the cure is commercial: learn to spin sugar from blood, and this scar sells itself.

III. Cookie Dough

Smart now, I coo on cue and echo mushy sound bites. Every kid knows undercooked goodies are sweetest, so I pick a make-me-up stick that says: tap my gooey center and sieve out my cute icky. Sex is food, and I practice wooing on myself—pig out then dig out the excess to leave my pout underfed. Men hungry for girls choke on my come-hither finger too.

They sniff my virginity ruse baked into a prepubescent essence, but they forget to time my reckless rising.

IV. Fanta Orange

What the nuns should have told us: agents of rot hype a fang as sweet tooth. It's always the bubbly ones who shake me, sugared on sex and ego. Head fizzed to bitsy this time, I feel fit with a buzz and a clit, but my fountain's open—hooch unguarded on the counter. Sparkler throat to aorta sputter: in minutes I'm a goner, stoking the flame on low. My ornate fantasy gamut ranges toe to ear, but blackout fantasia is rote the second time through, so I'll spare you the parts I don't know. Morning found me flat and tonguing a tang of old anger diffused.

V. Pink Lemonade

Having learned a limp tart is worse off, I reapply myself: string my bikini up with a snarl and paint my face in neon strips, Springer-prepped. Only some choices are limited. Boys take pokes at puckered hips while I temper my rage with manicured tips. Joy runs thin, but my flesh packs thick with pulpy trauma. I can peel it off in strips and watch my ugly sting them. Bitters on the eyelid, my leaky wounds pry like interviews—and just like that, the gawkers all sour on me. Boys and nuns in chorus sing: *put your clothes back on.* A dress code cracked: coverall as cover-up when violence is unsightly. So I skin myself feminine. A tall drink of raw pink, I'm the girliest yet. My girlhood is blistering.

EPISODE 3

The J Girls Give Face

(1998)

A Burlesque

EXT. BACKYARD – NIGHT. All five J GIRLS, wearing metallic bikinis, stand in an aboveground pool and swim-walk slowly around the edge, creating a whirlpool in the center. As each girl says her lines, she removes her top and then her bottom.

Pluralizing

JOCELYN: We blow cash on toe rings & studded spandex, then go all-pennies-in on who's first to leave the water undressed—

JODIE: or better yet: who's wet & naked longest. Watch: under pink-sky thunder, we pander to a stand of jeans & tall-boy cans. Six-packed into the tiny vinyl pool, we're nothing

JENNIFER: if not a fashioned set, weaving knees & elbows in a cat's cradle of regrets. O audience,

JACQUI: don't think we can't hear the storm coughing our names through the streets as window women shut their eyes to us. Don't assume we can't see from here

JOELLE: how many selves we'll have to synchronize in making sense of nights like this. Our love of leering men.

JOCELYN: *Poor* is an easy place to sink—*trashy*, too, but surfacing alone is a risk not one of us is taking.

JODIE: Not one & not none. When lightning scatters itself on the skin of the water, we crystallize with laughter. Our bodies' fractal tugs of longing split the clouds. We rip the light

JENNIFER: & wrap our hips
in it. We sieve the sky into our lips. We tilt the kaleidoscope
eye of sex so you can see it:

JACQUI: girl as gift, but in plural we're a
performance—*girls, girls, girls!* Lit now, translucent men call
from the deck: *crazy sluts,* so we slip

JOELLE: their words over our
heads & climb out cloaked in their dazzling fear of us. We
shiver & drip & glisten & pull the ladder up.

Monologue: Jacqui

INT. MALL – NIGHT. JACQUI sits at a table in a crowded food court. Behind her: Orange Julius, Sbarro, Charley's Subs, and an empty storefront. JODIE sits behind her facing the camera and suggestively moves a Blow Pop into and out of her mouth.

Mall Haunts

Born at the food court's dead end, we spit
our gum-chewed brains on the pavement
and cultivate a hollow gaze. We make ourselves

dead ringers for Dum Dums with our sticky
grab-me legs and polished bauble heads.
Inside, we're rotten as our mothers guess,

black hearts spongy with soft-core decadence.
We gild our gory parts with peach and glitter,
but corpsy flesh peeks through in streaks

and lacquer chips. Men circle at the restrooms,
sniffing decay in our gloss-peeled lips.
Eager flies abound. Fauxblivious, we claw

shop racks and moan, shine-hungry fanatics
who proffer tongues like zombies, a possum play
to ward off predatory *Heys*. Sometimes all

we find is fear—but it makes a slimming bind
as lining, or a gorgeous drape, so we wear it
home and call ourselves drop-dead.

Monologue: Jocelyn

INT. HALLWAY – DAY. JOCELYN stands in a doorway, her cleavage and shoulders heavily coated in gold body shimmer. Behind her, a full-length mirror in the bedroom partially reflects JOELLE recording.

Glitter Ode

Loyal decoy, you mimic
    tongue flickers & slick us
all over, no risk of drips
    or downers. Useless alone, you suck
our darkness in & let us sway
    in plural, where spectacle lies.
Flip bitch, you let us play
    our gold doubles & we waste no lays
of eyes. At the mall, at the pool,
    in study hall & Sunday school,
we're a chain of kinks that work
    ourselves out in slow motion.
But for now, you let us live
    as only shifting surfaces, brilliant
as a hoax, a hex, a hemorrhage
    of light. Fickle safety net, you trap
& fling the world from our skin.

Monologue: Jodie

EXT. COUNTY FAIRGROUNDS – DAY. Smoking a cigarette as she speaks, JODIE walks slowly down the center steps of an outdoor stadium, toward the camera. She is wearing men's clothing: baggy jeans, an Ohio State Buckeyes T-shirt, and a backward baseball cap.

Demolition Derby Queens

Come find us in the stadium with our polished fingers in our ears, teenage menthol dears without a fig to prove. We pick our favorite cars by color while men parrot engines, knowing jeers and revs will bore the skirts right off us. Beer foams down the bleachers, bathing our sandaled feet.

A belch of dirt ascend from the track, and we squint through it for the drama—a mangled wreck of rust and mud looks up, tragic as a soap opera death scene. Our squealing men have never been so sentimental, so glamorous in their rage—mine spent six weeks dolling up his beater, spray-painting my cartoon face on its hood, christening it with my name. A real trauma pageant, this big boys' game—a way of trading places.

When a zebra-painted Caprice rams my man, I shove my hand halfway down my jeans. I could come as he offs himself in a metal me—but he guns it straight onto the grass and leaves me hanging low in black bellies of smoke as we watch the finale: wrecked derby queens dragged from the track, snag-lipped with loose bumpers and spewing gasoline. We try our best to mimic their wounded sneering as we sulk home, girls on parade.

Shame Soap: Jennifer

MONTAGE. Shots of cityscape and items described with VO from JENNIFER.

Dangling Modifier

hey champ: inviting as tango: more mask than line: greased grip as cue: pool stick oversized: mean throat-music: white on white: a necklace of *good olds*: tongue bronzed in cheek: a lickle lime-bit: a curly lip: hidden flair: sucking exuberance: decorative dip: doily of spit: lace on pink corners: tough-shit theatrics: a light fixture of questions: intricate skirting: easy answer: arm garnished with breasts: thin slice of a wife: side-wedged: waitress-eyed: icy tip: lame dart: an off aim: a tail chase: a cock race: skull-cum-cage: hormone corset: socked in a soft place: verve made verbless: smile-mauled face: coal-black lid: mascara of manhood: a *lie back now*: climc of steep breaths: body as stage: other as exit

Monologue: Jacqui

INT. BASEMENT – DAY. Facing camera, JACQUI walks on a treadmill surrounded by cardboard boxes, a purple beanbag chair, and piles of clothing and shoes.

Ponytail Politic

Variety is coin for broke girls, so we count our options
and others', taking care to peep which kinky puckers
beckon with cinched breath, which slick founts open
wide for lush tides, and which bright orbs burst forth
then fade into empty space like ancient stars, centers

expanding with self-doubt. Perfection is a certain death
we'll never get with overfluffed cream puffs teasing
illusions of grandeur, so we resolve to dissolve ourselves
into our combs each night as we pray against morning's
worst fate: slivers limp and tonguely as tsking teachers.

To take our tails as ogled pawns in gravity's gambit
is to ignore the sex and ire that skitter down our spines.
More than accessory: we wear the shouts we're made
to swallow on our heads—tiny explosions gathered,
paused, and perched at our bodies' uppermost limits.
We can adjust these lithe lust toggles to watch boys

seethe for us. We know love's glacial swish is nothing
so nice as desire's nervy switch. It sets us ticking
like hallway metronomes clocking our unsung motto:
all hail feminine frivolity, most dangerous in numbers.
In endless rows of treadmill pendulums, we walk
a ticktock to silently say: *Our time is coming. Any day.*

> JACQUI *(pressing buttons on treadmill)*: *What the fuck?*
> JODIE *(OC)*: *Oh, it's broke. Just jump off.*
> JACQUI: *Jump where?*

Monologue: Joelle

INT. SCHOOL RESTROOM – DAY. JOELLE, wearing a plaid uniform skirt and white polo shirt, stands in front of a sink with her back to a mirror.

Cunts in the Girls' Room

We rule this muggy vestibule of ringed hands
cupped under faucets and caked wet cheeks.
Excess is catechism in the room that drinks

the runoff of girls made from too much—
cunts who push our luck with wobbly locks
we trust to keep our splitting bodies hidden

while we kiss and puke and cry and scratch
our names into the flaking paint. Neglected bins
spit towels and blood-soaked tampons on the tile

while we toe around and spritz our necks
vanilla to cloak the smoke or bile. We blow
the bell and lipstick stall. We all would kill

for another minute here alone—to study
our extra selves in the sunless mirror,
to find in our faces just one thing worthy.

Monologue: Jocelyn

INT. SCHOOL RESTROOM – DAY. JOCELYN, in a school uniform, stands in a front of a bathroom stall as she unfolds a piece of loose-leaf paper and reads from it.

oo-yay & eye-yay

ay-hey irl-gay

ets-lay o-gay
oo-tay all-way art-may
& et-gay um-say
op-pay & um-gay

ee-pay es-yay:
or-yay eye-may ush-cray

of-lay
or-yay irl-gay

Commercial Break: Joelle & Jocelyn

INT. BEDROOMS – NIGHT. JOELLE and JOCELYN appear in separate but consecutive clips, each girl painting her nails. They are not in the same place, but their parts are spliced together here.

Wet n Wild Romance

I. Putting on Airs: Joelle

I masc my femme with throaty guff, the better to hiss you with. Inhaling is a way to play gruff with the boys, tearing out giggles till I hone my voice swiss-like. They make a lingo of coughs and grunts designed to shut me out or up, but I trim my fearskin, shed the practiced frills, and prop my maw wide, holler outsized. I talk enough hot trash to melt a menthol in my mouth, and they shut trap. If listened to, boys will be ploys for detention, so I focus on flak. I mistress their brand of smoke and mirrors so well I don't have to drop trou to impress you.

II. Tickled Pink: Jocelyn

Soon I see you eye my glossies. You know my gorge is endless and takes praise by invitation only. Flattery proves gladder from girls who know what looking's for. Sick of sex as graceless ballet so come cradle this too-too face. I hold in my hand this would that I could sit cheek to cheek, mouth to mouth, tongue to flowering. You're thick with shine but give way like bit lip, tacky under thumb. Then you're my tucked-away chaser for weeks, my soft candy glaze, a dose of blush behind the tough, my finishing touch.

III. Blazed: Joelle

I walk you off at night—time-kill as cardio to watch unwanted thoughts melt away. In daylight, I hide them like blisters in my grimy jellies and get high to play safe. Sappy insists on negligence, so I hit hard to stay gay. (Oh, you didn't know? J/k. It's always the other kind of gay—not happy, but the kind you can wipe off in the mirror and say *j/k.*) See, you live just a joke away. I follow this flame to your house, where we quiz each other on boys and get blunt enough for shotgun games: Breathe fire into my throat so I can give it back to you. Blow quick before the world can Cosmo the last of this queer from our lips.

EPISODE 4

The J Girls Get Caught (on Camera)
(1998)

Interview: Anonymous Woman

INT. SCHOOL RESTROOM – DAY. ANONYMOUS WOMAN stands in front of a mirror and speaks to the camera through it.

VO: According to People magazine, a fifteen-year-old girl allegedly "had sex with multiple partners in a high school bathroom earlier this month, sparking an investigation by police and hundreds of news stories."

Documentary

There was a camera, which made it a dare—one good for sharing. So it looked like you took it, easy as pressing a button, bright red and round and begging. There was a camera, which made a number like *two dozen* concrete as pie. As if you wanted a prize. *Unaware*, some said—an easier story. There was a camera, which made it a story. The hour ate your beginning, middle, and end in perfect order. *Tasteless*, some said, but the camera made it a scene set with a blanket of pinkish spittle and knees bent like parentheses. Your life was a smudge on the lens that made the room into a U—a stall any *you* could fit into. The camera didn't blink as it drove itself into you. Maybe there was a point when you had to leave the room, so you just swallowed it, and then the room was you. All your breaths heaved in the vents. All your mouths foamed in the corners. All your heads sparked and shattered and nobody could see.

But there was still a camera, which kept insisting on objectivity, saying: *a cage made of arms is a cage no matter what the arms are doing.* Later, some wanted to comfort you, to share your grief like a sundae. A thousand mouths like parentheses, holding the excised bits. Bite-sized details like maraschino cherries, bright red and round and begging. There was a camera, after all, which chewed you into a thousand tiny truths.

Monologue: Jacqui

EXT. CORNER STORE – DAY. JACQUI paces outside a convenience store as she speaks. A sign on the door behind her reads, "Sam's Kwik Mart."

What the Thief Learned to Take Early

a naked picture in the skinny mirrors of a Sears dressing room
a minute to hit Send at home while wearing my new free clothes
a joke at school the next day about a bulldog eating mayonnaise
a bit off the top of my dumb cloudhead
a seat in any lap that opened like an eye on me, finally
a hit of almost anything without inhaling
a look in my mother's skull that opens each night like a Fabergé egg
a lift in the dark from women only
a big swig by the third time a friend told me I was more fun drunk
a second one before stuffing mini Mad Dog bottles like a litter of puppies,
    gently, into my purse
a bow when the cops opened my shirt to search for drugs or dirt
a break from self-pity when they didn't try to kill me
a half-educated guess as to whose world it really was
a test in how to stay warm without getting close to a soul
a deep breath before saying my name so it might blow open like a coat
    and reveal me
a hike across town to meet a man and shove the whole night in my mouth
a risk in the name of a boy whose love was small enough to get lost inside
    a condom
a shot at a clay pigeon with a face that opened like a burst of
    disappointment in my chest
a pill to bleed the baby out
a seat at the clinic when it didn't work
a quiz: which mistakes are cumulative?

Monologue: Jodie

INT/EXT. TACO BELL DRIVE-THRU WINDOW – NIGHT. JODIE, in a Taco Bell uniform shirt, leans out the window, facing the camera. She holds a sour cream gun in her right hand and periodically pumps it into the air for emphasis.

Viral

Danger is as danger and I once did—
working in a Taco Bell's warm-breath cloud
of spiced beef and tube cheese—
boob-flash a stunned mother
waiting at the drive-thru window,
mouth wide as a hungry suckling's.
Soon I saw all the PTA ma'ams
clutching their jumbo pearls, *as if*
I'd filch them from their chests.
My gall and glands were nothing
but appetizers for them. What whet lips
can spread: food, blood, spit, sweat.
Plus lube and pubes, uppers and cankers,
Fire Sauce even. Fastest are hisses and digs:
*Who knows what drugs she's on, how many
men.* So no need for DNA revenge—
trash that I am, my name passed tit to lip
through every throat in town by week's end.

Monologue: Jennifer

INT. CHURCH – DAY. JENNIFER sits in an empty church pew. Her makeup is color-coordinated with the stained-glass window behind her depicting the Virgin Mary: blue eyeliner, yellow eye shadow, white lipstick.

Prayer for Exposure

O my hallowed CAT scan, my x-ray of hope,
my moral microscope, my consecrated blood draw,
my pious pee test, my forensic father almighty,
my soul-seeking sleuth, my perpetual black light,
my sublime radar, my most private eye of eyes,
my silent paparazzo, my righteous nanny cam,
my reverse peephole, my sudden curtain pull,
my Maglite in the back alley of bedtime prayers,
my spiritual lockpick, my sacred search warrant,
my heavenly two-way mirror, my holy wiretap,
my giant ear to the wall of this profane heart,
my magnificent magnifying glass, my magic decoder—
look quick while I write all my sins on my skin
with the disappearing ink of your forgiveness.

Monologue: Jacqui

EXT. PLANNED PARENTHOOD – DAY. JACQUI stands on a walkway in front of the clinic. A man, a woman, and a teen boy stand a few yards back, holding signs and occasionally shouting at no one in particular.

Ode to an Empty Womb

O shrine of no miracle,
offering brood blood
unblessed into wine
on a shitty Friday night,
praise be for no godseed
bedding down in your pink tuck.

>   *PROTESTING MAN: Repent!*

No alien kick, no rabbit thump,
no scratchy whir and hum.
No cards from anybody.
I'm eating for one—
and you're a cold bowl of nothing,
my favorite unlunch.

>   *PROTESTING BOY: God loves you!*

Dark cubby, how many times
have I tried to scare loose
some ghost of self from you?
Monthly you hushed my terror,
and once, I scraped the shush
from your pried mouth.
No cry came out.

PROTESTING MAN: (unintelligible)

Shook pocket, you're all
mine now—a joyful void I carry
like the lightest clutch,
not one bright penny inside it.

Shame Soap: Jennifer

MONTAGE. Close shots of items described with VO from JENNIFER.

Double Negative

mine wasn't a pot not got: no gnat-filled grot: no pebble unturned: but you queried my quarry: how many untarpings before you: not silly to assume I wasn't an unhot lot: not a non grata: I wasn't unblissed: my lips weren't ungorgeous: but it wasn't the right box: some hole bored of us: not long & hand-mouth trysts began: a fist can be a stopper too: an answer: knock-knock: who's there: me, dressed in a houndstooth bruise: gum gaps as lack-clock: talk-talk: measure of nots: when it stops, the length of you: rage as distance unclosed: tied onto me: an unreminder too: how fast a not-you becomes a not-I: a knocked eye: my head not quite an unempty room: who's not always there: not me: not without you

Monologue: Joelle

INT. BEDROOM – NIGHT. JOELLE sits on an unmade bed holding a baby doll.

Mimi

mirrored my idea of baby me. Chatty doll double
of no self I could see, her pink bloomers and O lips

smacked of midwestern silence. At night, my breath
cauled her plastic skull and fogged her one stuck-open eye,

its blue glass a tiny rupture in the black room. Funny
how a doll can only look reciprocally.

Pregnancy crazed, I shoved a balled Mimi up my shirt
when I fell asleep, but later I left her splayed

in the corner as porn taught me the right way
to give a blow job. The kneeling woman on-screen

had brown hair like mine, but I couldn't see her face,
by which I mean: she couldn't look back at me. I won't

say this is why I kept quiet when a boy filled his hands
with my body in the chapel after school one day. But

I will tell you he never once looked at my face or saw
the bright rupture of rage under my tongue. When I spoke

out of turn in class after that, the nuns asked: *Who
do you think you are?* I thought of Mimi's worn-out voice box

bleating *me me*, an echo of her original plea: *kiss me—*
dumb doll who could only name herself by breaking.

(Camera is set on the ground.)

JODIE *(OC): Just so you know, I don't care.*
JOELLE *(OC): About what?*
JODIE *(OC): You and Jocelyn or whatever.*
JOELLE *(OC): What about us?*
JODIE *(OC, after a beat): Never mind.*

Commercial Break: Jocelyn

EXT. PORCH – DUSK. JOCELYN sits on a stoop with four nail polish bottles in front of her feet. As she says the name of each color, she picks up the corresponding bottle and sets it behind her.

Avon Grotesque

I. Ruby Slippers

So American, my pleasure in getting took. One giddy heel-snap had my hands and eyes packed for a love who dropped me miles past gone.

A rube in rook shoes, I walked some change loose, found kin in the suburbs of rose-papered windows—yuppies like getting took too. So femme, their optimism.

Right off, Sylvie, the gaudy priss-dealer to all the block moms, high-robbed me for red press-ons. Godless and hungry, I clung like a charm to her purse, supped on her uppers, and sunk into piles of polish and wax and glue.

No place like out-from-under, as Sylvie sung. So Hollywood, her largesse. Houseshod, I became her delivery pet: supplier and supplicant, superb subterfuge.

II. Golden Vision

A girlhood lobbying for ungot baubles prepped me for hawking little pots of gold. Sylvie was a con who mommed me under winged eyelids, but it came with training:

my inborn corneal spectrum of pinks projected as swindler's optimism. I sold while Sylvie softened her edge and junked up on catchpennies.

Soon I got myself a bevy and said to them: a rosy face suggests a better place—manifest besting of self. Service is easy: mine your p's and q's for capital from lower cases. Look at me: pawn turned queen.

Good little bets, they believed me. So I built myself a woman tower made of lips and eyes and toes: from the ground up, a roundup of women buying women buying woman suits.

III. Lucky Penny

As suckers would have it, pluck alone wins trust and coins. Slick sellers tell it worse. Sylvie said to worth your customers—

you have to halve them based on buys: blues and whites on eyes go right, nudes on nails go left; poor puts on a show, subtle means rich if it takes three coats.

A fickle trickle-down, though: my numbers rose like skirts when I clowned my lash and pout, as if fate spit me out their luckpoor polish girl.

Money loves talk of change from within, so I swallowed their bills and chased success tales. Sylvie retired with a closet of free bronzer and ten USA pins.

IV. Decadence

A decade deals a hundred folds, but I flat my bills in a stack of catalogs while narrative looms. How long till up-and-coming becomes comeuppance—

rouge rots to goo and lacquer dries to glass. Sylvie's product motto: *Nothing old can stay.* Even her mind in the end flaked away.

So no coddling twilight. My long-term is to ward off wear by dipping out young and donning all my stock into the ground. Paint me into a stunning ghoul: purple tips, cerulean lips, lids a neon jaundice. Name it *Death Rococo.*

Better still: skip the formaldehyde and fill me with glitter. When they dig me up to clear a Walmart lot, imagine the beauty they'll find.

EPISODE 5

The J Girls Reunion
(2000)

Y2K Confessions

INT. SCHOOL GYMNASUM – NIGHT. A stage is set with five chairs. JENNIFER, who is dressed as a nun, and JOCELYN, who is wearing a bikini, are seated to the right of JACQUI, who wears a fake beard and a suit. JOELLE is seated to the left of JACQUI. Next to JOELLE is an empty chair, behind which is a narrow door. In view is a CROWD of four people seated in folding chairs in front of the stage.

BEARDED JACQUI: On today's show: Girls and sex—are they having it? Let's find out. Our first guest is back from the suburbs to declare her love for . . . her ex-*girl*friend.

CROWD *(cheers)*

BEARDED JACQUI: But the ex says nothing ever happened! Jocelyn and Joelle, who's telling the truth? Have you had sexual relations? Or is this allegation an inflation of purely platonic relations?

JOELLE: It was just a phase. I'm not in the closet.

JOCELYN *(adjusting bikini strap)*: But *we* were. It was heaven every time we did it in a closet.

CROWD *(cheers)*

JOELLE: Well, I must be misremembering something. Seven minutes to *come too* or *come to*?

CROWD *(jeers)*

JOCELYN: We certainly weren't taught the difference in school.

CROWD *(boos)*

JOELLE: Sometimes girl on girl means swapping rape stories.

CROWD *(boos)*

BEARDED JACQUI: A question from the crowd—yes, ma'am?

ANONYMOUS WOMAN *(stands)*: I don't think they did have sex—not fully—because what can two girls really do, you know? *(sitting down)* I wanna know what they can do.

CROWD *(boos)*

BEARDED JACQUI: Interesting point. So what you're saying is it depends on what the definition of *is* is. *(turning to Joelle)* Is *is*, in this case, really *is*—or is *is* only as *is* does? And what is it that *is* does, in this case?

HECKLER: Yeah, what's the good stuff?

JENNIFER *(chewing nail)*: That's disgusting.

JOCELYN: So holy! I saw you kneeling in front of someone who didn't look like Jesus.

CROWD *(laughs)*

JOCELYN *(crosses arms)*: Looked like Mr. Peters from algebra.

BEARDED JACQUI: Jodie, is this belated revelation a veracious and bona fide datum? Have you fellated someone other than our Lord and Savior?

JENNIFER *(looking down)*: God—d—d—d—

(tape glitches)

CROWD *(applauds)*

BEARDED JACQUI: I see. Jocelyn, you've called yourself *bisexual*; would you say you were *booorn* this way?

JOCELYN: Like a disease they can't get? *(gestures to CROWD)*

CROWD *(boos)*

HECKLER: So you still fuck men?

BEARED JACQUI: Speaking of men—Joelle, we do have some evidence that you've pleasured fellows in your residence, including, I believe, a stained dress? Your sister tells us this behavior has been prevalent since adolescence.

CROWD *(cheers)*

JOELLE *(rolls her eyes)*

BEARDED JACQUI: We actually have your sister backstage with us today.

CROWD *(gasps)*

BEARDED JACQUI: Jodie, come on out!

CROWD *(jeers)*

JODIE *(emerges from behind the narrow door and struts across stage with her arms outspread, smiling)*

JODIE *(sitting down and gesturing toward JOELLE)*: Just like a Libra—she never could make a decision.

CROWD *(boos)*

BEARDED JACQUI: Joelle, let's cut through the fray. Why don't you tell us right here if your affair was simply an act of play or if you were seductively led astray?

JODIE: She's always been afraid. In school, the nuns would slap her left palm when she wrote with it, and then she'd come home and wet the bed.

JOELLE: They slapped yours too.

JODIE: Yeah, but I'm still left-handed.

CROWD *(jeers)*

JOELLE *(flips off CROWD)*

BEARDED JACQUI *(stroking her beard)*: Is that a yay or a nay to the question of being gay?

JOELLE: It's not a big deal. I'm telling you—it's just not.

CROWD *(boos)*

JOELLE: It's not a big telling. It's just—

(tape glitches)

JOELLE: Telling deals a big knot.

CROWD *(boos)*

JOELLE: It's telling I'm not.

CROWD *(boos)*

JOELLE: It's a big big.

CROWD *(boos)*

JOELLE: I'm just.

CROWD *(boos)*

JOELLE: Not not.

EPISODE 6

The J Girls Cash Out

(2000)

Interview: Anonymous Woman

INT. BEDROOM – MORNING. ANONYMOUS WOMAN stands in front of a window, backlit from outdoor light so that it's difficult to see her features clearly.

Selfward

In one life, I was a mail-order house
with a picture window for a mouth.

Every sigh hit with a thud; every word
was a spot of blood on the glass.

If you looked closely, you could see inside:
my sex on a table like a porcelain bowl

refilled & refilled. I sold myself. The deed
was a wad of pink gum stuck beneath

that table for thirty years. You understand:
there was no doer & there was no door.

Call me a ward of the state of things—
a call girl, a girl to be called *girl*. We all were

bound for wealth. We all dressed ourselves
with names & lips like awnings.

Each man stood on his sex like a scaffold,
holding a brush & a bucket of blue.

Monologue: Jocelyn

INT. KITCHEN – DAY. JOCELYN sits at the table wearing a red apron, a plate of cookies in front of her. A dog can be heard barking from another room.

Silence Is Golden—

a scold not beholden to trite mothers
or regret-tongued nuns, who teach us to never appear
as smart as a man, because a bird in the fist
is worth the whole wedding. Find bliss in spilled milk,
they say—ignorance is an upper hand.
How's the rest? Catch more men with the honey jar open
& a bed soaked in vinegar is a woman's work
never done by a girl well-begun who's only half-fun.
But good things come to those who flock together,
who pluck their own feathers & stock their pots
with bad weather. So never pick up stones
you can't throw, never count your bones in the bathwater
& never keep your babies in glass houses.
If you don't have anything nice to say, for God's sake,
don't lead a gift horse to your mouth.
Look, don't beat a dead bliss—a hitch in time saves tears
down the line. Besides, one idle hand
will just watch the other clench up. Remember:
the devil is in a detailed disguise.

Monologue: Jodie

INT. KITCHEN – DAY. JODIE stands in front of a stove, a saucepan on a burner behind her. A Minnie Mouse dish towel is draped over her shoulder. She smokes a cigarette from a long holder, periodically ashing into the saucepan. A dog is still barking in another room.

I Could Eat You Up

Something other in heels is a meal
    for glutting—romance be damned—
so I'm yours, other enough for a night.
    Maybe you think me a cheap chick:
don't mind the zip ties & I skip your good wine.
    My champ-mouth runs foul with beer
& a bit of old pride, so the fantasy lives:
    by midnight I'm raring, aping a fit,
but you suspect I'll bag nice & sleazy after a hunt.
    Having learned desire will fork at the pit
of tenderness, you pull back a wrist to buffet
    & bowl me over. I fawn & you buy it,
hooked on the lure of taming a challenge.
    You ought to know better ways
of penning a girl into a story, but I play along
    to groom myself sportive. So fire me up—
cleaved or hung, it's all game for a buck.
    Some men curry a compromise,
meting out sweetness—but not you:
    I'm steered & pinned. In turn,
I give tail & trail your yelps to let you believe
    I love it—as if your need sates me,
as if one hunger just swallows the other.

Shame Soap: Jennifer

MONTAGE. Shots of house interior and items described with VO from JENNIFER.

Circular Argument

ring, an opening: I birthed him a wedding: little gold garter: called it my honesty belt: my tiny God conduit: short-circuited hand: a waiting mouth: my shout-binky: a forget-me knot: a bird's-eye target: an invitation: *O* marks the spot

spot as wound: ring around the floozy: the room was open-ended: I flew across it for miles: cop called it a doozy: knew I'd copped a meal before: we shopped a deal: he popped a seal: his teeth had silver linings: lips ready: I faltered to feel: cop called it a *face-to-wall* deal: the room ended then

then more questions: I was peppered: a heart steak: a dark walk: a hard break: the surface of the lake ramified me too: I ate my reflection: an about-face: *it's about place,* he said: mine was at the bottom: a fish-eye view: the sun above a tiny ring

Monologue: Jacqui

EXT. FRONT PORCH – DUSK. JACQUI sits on a glider, fanning herself with a spread of Snoopy playing cards. JODIE sits next to her with a pile of one- and five-dollar bills on her lap.

Who Taught You That One?

My mother's one lesson: waste not your wild card
on kiddie bits for broke boys; love pays like jack shit.

Come hither the din of my siren tongue & I hone
a slip-slither, all leg in winter, all wadded-up cup.

Just a sorry spine inside a halter, she says: a diamond-
cut to curb my low-high swerve & I break like a mirror.

But a sticky hand can't dither—I gather the dark in her
voice & tar my lips with it, easy ticket to summon

old detention dreams: come hither the floor
to my knees, the cracked lip of a wallet to part my teeth

& make a man call the ceiling *baby*. A domino job,
they all fell for me. I summon my mother's memory:

her pee-stick-in-the-Kool-Aid trick suckered in cash
vacuum-quick—her baby-blue ruse, never even a man in her

own bed & still we ate French: tarte tatin, coq au vin, mille-feuille.
She taught me to rob the bank of the body. So I suffer

the rich men to come unto me. I suffer their groan-
mouths to open & now who's whose little suckling?

Ears to my chest, they can't hear the train for the track—
the girl who cries *baby*. Beneath a greased veil of breath,

I trace my millefleur eyelids & count: all mine is their kingdom.

Monologue: Joelle

INT. BEDROOM – NIGHT. JOELLE sits cross-legged on a waterbed with no sheets, wearing a bra with boxer shorts and holding a cordless phone in her lap.

Can I Call You Ellie?

Call me Ellie with the jelly lip. Sad-Sour Ellie

with hog-tied thighs. Blissed Ellie with piss on the tip

of her canines. Always coddled a shine for the dirty,

so call me Ellie the Flirt & don't bother to wake me

from my shake-dreams. Dogged eye trained on Ellie

the Bite Sleeve, your peek-tongue grin bets you'll call me

Ellie Broke-Legs, Ellie Moan-Pays, Ellie Tuck-Teeth or else

Whistle-Gum, Ellie Licks-a-Lesson-in-Her-Blood. Fist-turn

the dough of me to Ellie the Grateful. Ellie Sock Full

o' Change, my head full o' throwaway games. Turn me down

to the stuffing & call me Ellie No-Face. Your soft Shellie

No-Place. Oh-God-Oh-God-Ellie, who eats up God's grace.

On Ellie the Shoulder you pray to Ellie Who Has No Name—

save for Ellie the Warm Trap where hope lays.

Monologue: Jocelyn

INT. MCDONALD'S – DAY. JOCELYN sits in a booth. A customer and several employees can be seen watching from the counter behind her.

McDonald's 4-ever

I want to wade there with you on a snow day,
    wheeze-winded & teary. I want to smash the ice
in your lashes, then let the oily steam breathe us
    back to running blood. Or I want to walk there
in crop tops we'll swap in the lime fluorescence
    of the slime-tiled john so we can walk home as one
another. I want to wooze in your menthol-cherry
    aura as we find every flickering arch in the city.

> *CASHIER: Double-cheeseburger meal,*
> *order two-oh-nine.*

Delicate licker of grease-dipped french tips,
    send me a Rite Aid valentine that says *be my bitch*
& I'll be yours. No takebacks, no beef, no joke, no jinx
    when I answered that trick crush question with *you*—
you who then flipped & tramped the whole year solo.

> *CASHIER (annoyed): Order two-oh-nine,*
> *double cheeseburger.*

    But I swear on your stuck-up spine we can walk
it all back with Big Macs & a thousand half-hug pats.
    Please let's just meet on the mouth of a straw,
suck it up, crush only our cups & let the years drip down
    the sewer slats as we walk back & back & back.

End Credits

EXT. STREET – DUSK. Shaky continuous shot rolling down mixed residential-commercial street with call-and-response VO from all five J GIRLS.

Beatitudes for Meek Girls

Blessed is the bleached blonde pitching the parking-lot ballyhoo:
>She will wring a flask of joy from this wet-rag life before curfew.

Crowned is the cowgirl bucked from the club's mechanical bull:
>She will cull men like cattle and harness the sadness of fools.

Anointed is the pantyless mocktease hiking her skirt to her crotch:
>She will rub herself with prayer while the tongue-tskers watch.

Favored is the jilted teenager keying her man's Cavalier:
>She will carve the world's pearled concern down to a sneer.

Exalted is the halter-clad hustler working the skating rink john:
>She will bank her good looks and dumb luck till they're gone.

Redeemed is the sticky lamé queen with an O throat like a siren:
>She will curdle in urgent hands and stain every bed she lies in.

Holy is the pole-riding pip-squeak in pasties and a practiced pout:
>She will love the electric buzz of her name in a stranger's mouth.

Saved is the jailbait with the fake ID and a bartender friend:
>She will drop her head like a sinker and wait in the deep end.

Acknowledgments

I'd like to thank the institutions who've supported this project, including Yaddo, Vermont Studio Center, the University of Central Florida, and the University of Cincinnati, where this project began.

Special thanks to my mentors at UC who helped shape this book, especially Rebecca Lindenberg, Danielle Deulen, Don Bogen, John Drury, Beth Ash, and Jennifer Glaser. Thanks also to my friends from UC who've supported my work in and outside class.

I'm in debt to friends who've influenced this particular project and helped me conceptualize or revise its contents over the years: Lisa Summe, Madeleine Wattenberg, Sara Watson, Julia Koets, Lo Kwa Mei-en, Lauren Moseley, Joellen Craft, Ellen Bush, Bridget Bell, Sarah Huener, and Marlin Jenkins.

I'm grateful to my family and friends for their support, especially my mother, my stepfather, and my sister. Thank you to Emily for all her love and support. Thanks also to Doug for his support as I worked on this project. And thank you to all the Youngstown girls whose friendship helped shaped my adolescence.

Lastly, thank you to *Indiana Review*, Blue Light Books, Indiana University Press, and judge Nandi Comer for believing in my work. Thank you to Anni Jyn for her generosity and artwork. I'm grateful to everyone involved in bringing this book to life.

Credits

I'm grateful to these journals, who first published the following poems:

32 Poems: "Silence Is Golden—"

The Awl: "Wifebeaters"

Barrow Street: "Beatitudes for Meek Girls" and "Prayer for Effacement"

Bat City Review: "Selfward"

Bennington Review: "Thigh High" and "Prayer for Containment"

Crazyhorse: "Less Is More" as "Fourteen"

Cream City Review: "Demolition Derby Queens"

Diode: "Avon Grotesque"

Dream Pop: "Wet n Wild Romance"

Four Way Review: "McDonald's 4-ever" and "Ode on My Upspeak"

Glass Poetry: "Mimi"

Greensboro Review: "Weeknight"

Grist: "Double Negative" and "Prayer for Exposure"

Hayden's Ferry Review: "Documentary"

Hotel Amerika: "Bath & Body Works Pastoral" as "Teenage Pastoral"

Indiana Review: "Adoration of the J Girls"

The Journal: "Who Taught You That One?" and "Can I Call You Ellie?"

The Laurel Review: "Origins & Outcomes"

Memorious: "Ode to an Empty Womb"

Michigan Quarterly Review: "Mall Haunts"

New South: "I Could Eat You Up"

North American Review: "Ponytail Politic" as "Ponytail Ode"

Phoebe: "Pluralizing" as "Kaleidoscope"

Pleiades: "The Birth of Anger at the Roller-Skating Rink"

PRISM International: "Ode to the C Word"

Puerto del Sol: "Glitter Ode" and "Cunts in the Girls' Room"

Quarter After Eight: "Circular Argument" as "Pearl"

RHINO: "Middling"

Taco Bell Quarterly: "Viral" as "Hotcakes"

Third Coast: "Ode to My '81 Chevy Celebrity" as "Car Ode"

Tinderbox Poetry: "Lip Smacker Fantasia" and "The Cut" as "Poem for Lorena Bobbitt"

Rochelle Hurt is a poet and essayist. Her other books include *In Which I Play the Runaway* (Barrow Street, 2016), which won the Barrow Street Book Prize, and *The Rusted City: A Novel in Poems* (White Pine, 2014). Her work has been included in *Poetry* magazine and the *Best New Poets* anthology series, and she has been awarded prizes and fellowships from *Poetry International*, *Arts & Letters*, Vermont Studio Center, Jentel, and Yaddo. Originally from Youngstown, Ohio, she now lives in Orlando and teaches in the MFA program at the University of Central Florida.

Printed in the USA
CPSIA information can be obtained
at www.ICGtesting.com
LVHW071127310824
789806LV00010B/55

9 780253 060600